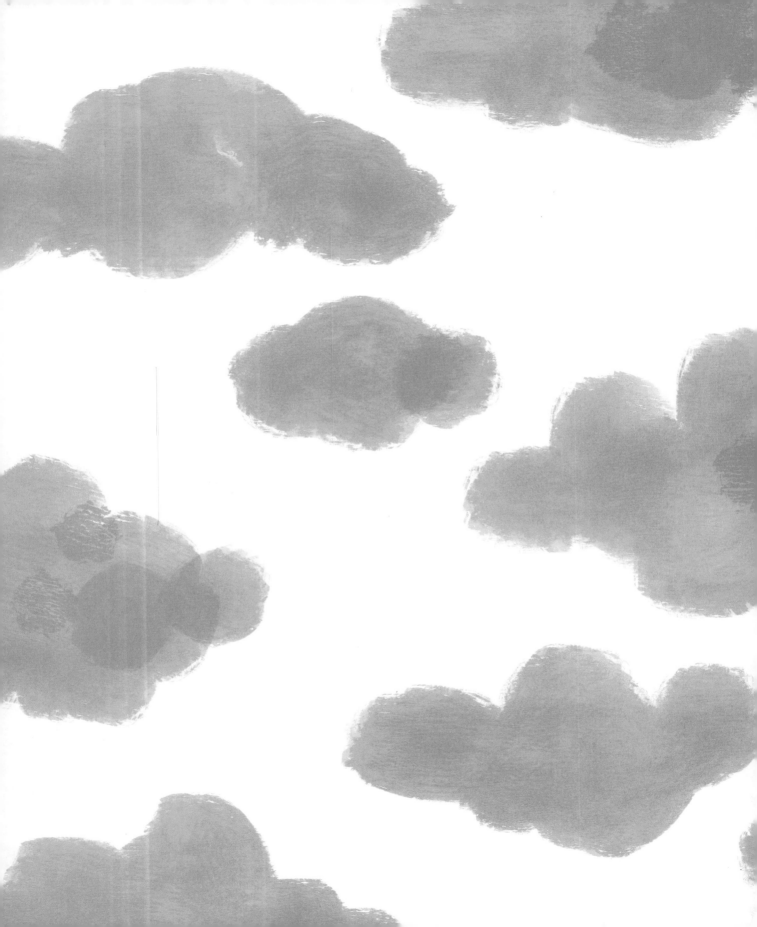

NOT ALL SHEEP ARE BORING!

Words by
Bobby Moynihan

Pictures by
Julie Rowan-Zoch

putnam

G.P. PUTNAM'S SONS

People count sheep to fall asleep.

But . . .

NOT ALL SHEEP ARE BORING!

I can prove it!

For example . . . This is Alice.
Alice has a jet pack. AND a helmet.

Because Alice is smart
AND cool. See?!
A sheep with a jet pack?!?
Alice is NOT boring!

This is Julie.
Julie likes dancing,
drinking coffee in the morning,
and then drinking more coffee
later in the morning.

I don't think Julie is boring
in the slightest. I love Julie.
And JULIE LOVES COFFEE!

This guy right here
is Mike H.
Mike H. really enjoys
pickles.
That's it. Just pickles.
Boring, you say?

Did I tell you Mike H. likes to eat pickles while sitting in a big wet boot?

Still boring?

This is Quinn.

Quinn owns several large hats.

Um . . . what else?

Oh! Quinn enjoys a slight wind
and also standing. That's cool . . . right?
Just standing there?

Definitely not boring
in any way? Right?

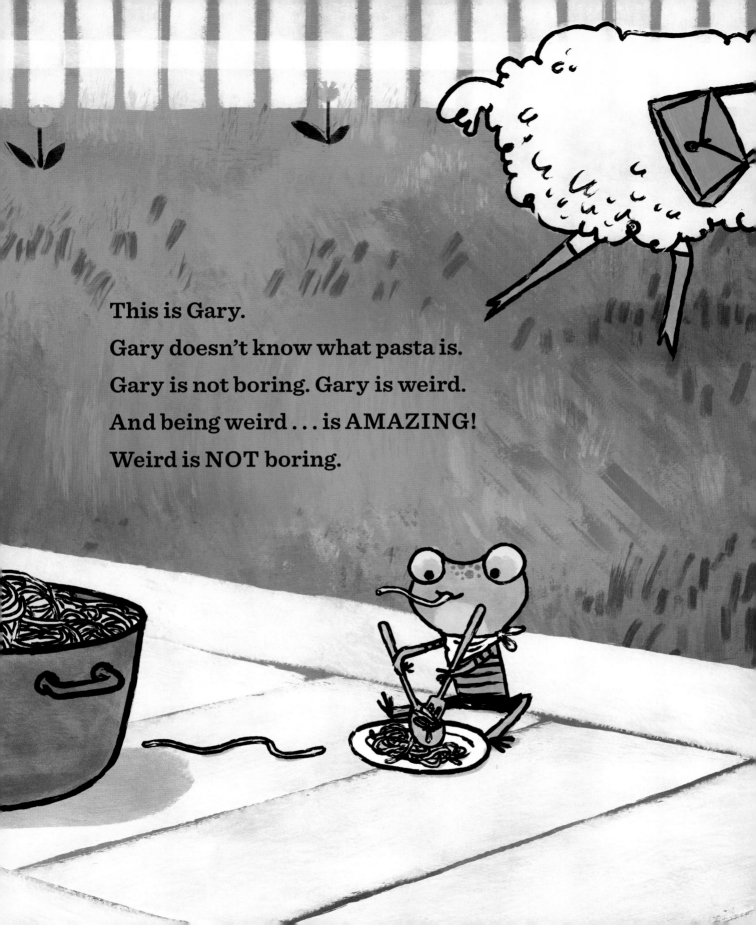

This is Gary.

Gary doesn't know what pasta is.

Gary is not boring. Gary is weird.

And being weird . . . is AMAZING!

Weird is NOT boring.

Look who it is! It's Marny!
Marny thinks it's rude to chew
with your mouth open.

Marny's right! Way to be, Marny!
Standing up for what
you think is right is NOT BORING!

Guess what?

DAN KEEPS BEES!!!
Is that boring?
I added three whole exclamation
points to make it sound more fun.
Too much???
Bees are awesome! Right?
Wait. Maybe it's Dan who's boring.
I blame Dan.

Whoa. Whoa. Whoa.

What in the who is this, now?

Wow. Well, she seems . . . VERY NOT BORING.

She seems like a lot of FUN?!?

Wait a second . . .

What if I told you that Katie was the first
sheep to ever prance on the moon?
Would you think that Katie was boring?
You wouldn't?
Great!

Buuuuuuut if I told you that,
I would be fibbing.
Katie has only pranced on Earth.
But maybe someday!

Oh boy.

It's Pierre.

Pierre. Has. Secrets.

Say hi to Jessica.

Jessica used to date Gary.

The sheep from before who didn't know
what pasta was?

But they broke up.

Not because he was boring.

BECAUSE JESSICA LOVES PASTA!!!

BUT NOT ALL SHEEP ARE GARY!!!

And then there's Steve . . .

Oof.
Steve.
Not gonna lie. Steve is
a little boring.

Steve's making me kinda tired.

Can you at least TRY to not be boring, Steve?

No?

Steve . . .

Oof.

Steve is very boring.

But . . . just because
Steve is EXTREMELY boring . . .

Always remember . . . that doesn't
mean . . . that ALL . . . sheep . . . are . . .
NOT . . . ALL . . . SHEEP . . . ARE . . .

Z Z Z Z Z z

For Dorothy. And Brynn. I love yee.
And Bimi and Bop.

And also the Coccos, Powells, Henrys,
Wantys, McNallys, Corderos, and O'Malleys.

Shoot. Can't forget Drowsus, Nugget, Melissa,
and Eli and Erika. Now I'm done.

Wait.

And Police Chief Rumble. That's it.

Wait.

And Keanu Reeves. THANK YOU, KEANU REEVES,
FOR ALWAYS BEING SO GREAT.
Oh! And Dave Goelz too. Love Dave. Okay. I'm done now.

No, I am not . . .

Thanks to George Lucas, the beverage Peach Snapple, and the television show *Lost*.
And to all my closest friends and loved ones . . . you will find you are all personally listed in large font at
peoplewhodidnotfitinthededicationofnotallsheepareboring.com.

But mostly for DOROTHY . . . and Carrie Fisher.

—Bibby

For my never-boring siblings,
Leslie and Richie.

—J. R.-Z.

G. P. PUTNAM'S SONS
An imprint of Penguin Random House LLC, New York
First published in the United States of America by G. P. Putnam's Sons, an imprint of Penguin Random House LLC, 2022
Copyright © 2022 by Bobby Moynihan
Penguin supports copyright. Copyright fuels creativity, encourages diverse voices, promotes free speech, and creates a vibrant culture.
Thank you for buying an authorized edition of this book and for complying with copyright laws by not reproducing, scanning, or distributing
any part of it in any form without permission. You are supporting writers and allowing Penguin to continue to publish books for every reader.
G. P. Putnam's Sons is a registered trademark of Penguin Random House LLC. | Visit us online at penguinrandomhouse.com
Library of Congress Cataloging-in-Publication Data | Names: Moynihan, Bobby, 1977– author. | Rowan-Zoch, Julie, illustrator.
Title: Not all sheep are boring! / by Bobby Moynihan; illustrated by Julie Rowan-Zoch. | Description: New York: G. P. Putnam's Sons, 2022.
Summary: "A bedtime book challenging the idea that sheep are boring enough to put you to sleep"—Provided by publisher.
Identifiers: LCCN 2021044361 (print) | LCCN 2021044362 (ebook) | ISBN 9780593407035 (hardcover) | ISBN 9780593407042 (epub)
ISBN 9780593407059 (kindle edition) | Subjects: CYAC: Sheep—Fiction. | LCGFT: Picture books.
Classification: LCC PZ7.1.M7287 No 2022 (print) | LCC PZ7.1.M7287 (ebook) | DDC [E]—dc23
LC record available at https://lccn.loc.gov/2021044361 | LC ebook record available at https://lccn.loc.gov/2021044362
Printed in the United States of America | ISBN 9780593407035 | 10 9 8 7 6 5 4 3 2 1 | PC
Design by Nicole Rheingans | Text set in Sentinel | The illustrations in the book were done on an iPad in Procreate.
The publisher does not have any control over and does not assume any responsibility for author or third-party websites or their content.